A Note to Parents and Caregivers:

Read-it! Readers are for children who are just starting on the amazing road to reading. These beautiful books support both the acquisition of reading skills and the love of books.

The PURPLE LEVEL presents basic topics and objects using high frequency words and simple language patterns.

The RED LEVEL presents familiar topics using common words and repeating sentence patterns.

The BLUE LEVEL presents new ideas using a larger vocabulary and varied sentence structure.

The YELLOW LEVEL presents more challenging ideas, a broad vocabulary, and wide variety in sentence structure.

The GREEN LEVEL presents more complex ideas, an extended vocabulary range, and expanded language structures.

The ORANGE LEVEL presents a wide range of ideas and concepts using challenging vocabulary and complex language structures.

When sharing a book with your child, read in short stretches, pausing often to talk about the pictures. Have your child turn the pages and point to the pictures and familiar words. And be sure to reread favorite stories or parts of stories.

There is no right or wrong way to share books with children. Find time to read with your child, and pass on the legacy of literacy.

Adria F. Klein, Ph.D.
Professor Emeritus
California State University
San Bernardino, California

To my big brother, and all my friends whose dads always have something to do ...

First American edition published in 2005 by
Picture Window Books
5115 Excelsior Boulevard
Suite 232
Minneapolis, MN 55416
877-845-8392
www.picturewindowbooks.com

First published in Canada in 2001 by
Les éditions Héritage inc.
300 Arran Street, Saint Lambert
Quebec, Canada J4R 1K5

Printed in the United States of America.

Library of Congress Cataloging-in-Publication Data
St-Aubin, Bruno.
Daddy's a busy beaver / written and illustrated by Bruno St-Aubin.
p. cm. — (Read-it! readers)
Summary: When their father becomes "a regular Mister Do-It-Yourself," his children wish
he had more time for them.
ISBN 1-4048-1025-0 (hardcover)
[1. Father and child—Fiction. 2. Building—Fiction.] I. Title: Daddy is a busy beaver.
II. Title. III. Series.

PZ7.S7743Dab 2004
[E]—dc22   2004023913

Daddy's a Busy Beaver

Written and Illustrated by
Bruno St-Aubin

Special thanks to our advisers for their expertise:

Adria F. Klein, Ph.D.
Professor Emeritus, California State University
San Bernardino, California

Susan Kesselring, M.A.
Literacy Educator
Rosemount - Apple Valley - Eagan (Minnesota) School District

PiCTURE WiNDOW BOOKS
Minneapolis, Minnesota

Before, Daddy looked like a dinosaur.

He was a little strange ... but pretty funny!

These days, he's really a busy beaver.

He's a regular Mister Do-It-Yourself.

Mommy thinks he's very handy.

He makes all sorts of gadgets.

In the summer, Daddy builds tree houses for my brother and me.

In the winter, he makes us igloos.

What we want to do is play with him.

But it's hopeless, because he's always too busy.

In the evening, Daddy reads piles of home repair magazines.

That's because he's planning some big
construction projects.

First, he draws plans. Then, he builds a model.

But he has trouble with the superglue!

He's better at electricity.

He can straighten his hair out in a flash!

Sometimes Daddy misses a nail and hits
his finger.

He gets mad and glares at us.

But he still manages to fix the roof of
our house.

Now it doesn't rain in our bedroom!

To thank Daddy,
we help him weed the garden.

But we're not supposed to talk to him.
He's too busy.

So then he goes and hides in his workshop ...

where he just works even harder!

That's when we decide to help him.

Poor Daddy! That upsets him even more!

My brother and I like dinosaurs and beavers.

But we like it best when Daddy is busy ...
with us!

More *Read-it!* Readers

Bright pictures and fun stories help you practice your
reading skills. Look for more books at your level.

Alex and the Team Jersey by Gilles Tibo
Alex and Toolie by Gilles Tibo
Clever Cat by Karen Wallace
Daddy's a Busy Beaver by Bruno St-Aubin
Daddy's a Dinosaur by Bruno St-Aubin
Felicio's Incredible Invention by Mireille Villeneuve
Flora McQuack by Penny Dolan
Izzie's Idea by Jillian Powell
Mysteries for Felicio by Mireille Villeneuve
Naughty Nancy by Anne Cassidy
Parents Do the Weirdest Things! by Louise Tondreau-Levert
Peppy, Patch, and the Postman by Marisol Sarrazin
Peppy, Patch, and the Socks by Marisol Sarrazin
The Princess and the Frog by Margaret Nash
The Roly-Poly Rice Ball by Penny Dolan
Run! by Sue Ferraby
Sausages! by Anne Adeney
Stickers, Shells, and Snow Globes by Dana Meachen Rau
Theodore the Millipede by Carole Tremblay
The Truth About Hansel and Gretel by Karina Law
Willie the Whale by Joy Oades

Looking for a specific title or level? A complete list
of *Read-it!* Readers is available on our Web site:
www.picturewindowbooks.com